To

Cooper and Quinn

From

G. Grandma Joan

and David

For Ellen Temple J.R.

Text by Mary Joslin

Published by Lion Children's Books
an imprint of
Lion Hudson plc
Wilkinson House, Jordan Hill Road,
Oxford OX2 8DR, England
www.lionhudson.com/lionchildrens

ISBN 978 0 7459 6299 3

First edition 2013

Acknowledgments
Bible retellings are based on the corresponding passages in the Good News Bible published by the Bible Societies and HarperCollins Publishers, © American Bible Society 1994, used with permission.

A catalogue record for this book is available
from the British Library

Printed and bound in China, June 2014, LH17

The Lion Classic

Christmas Stories

Retold by MARY JOSLIN

Illustrated by JANE RAY

LION
CHILDREN'S

Contents

The Nativity according to Saint Luke

The story of Jesus' Nativity is at the heart of Christmas. It is one that is known all over the world; yet it began very quietly, in a little corner of the Roman empire, in the time when Herod the Great was king of Judea.

To the north of Judea is a region known as Galilee. Olives and vines grow on its hilly slopes, and shepherds lead their flocks to graze the rough pasture. Among this farm country is a town named Nazareth, and this perfectly ordinary place was once home to a woman named Mary. At the time, people thought of her as a perfectly ordinary young woman. The man she was planning to marry had a more remarkable background; his family could trace their roots all the way back to the greatest king the Jewish nation had ever known: King David. However, all that was centuries in the past, and indeed everyone thought of Joseph as a perfectly ordinary man: the local carpenter.

Then the extraordinary happened. God sent the angel Gabriel to Nazareth to deliver a message to Mary.

It began in the customary way: "Shalom. Peace be with you."

Then it continued: "God is with you and has greatly blessed you."

Mary looked at the angel, her eyes betraying her disquiet. Who was it who had come from nowhere with such an unexpected message? What did it mean?

"Don't be afraid, Mary," said the angel. "God has chosen you to bear a child – a son. He will be known as the Son of the Most High God. He will be a king, greater than David of long ago, and his kingdom will never end."

The angel spoke with great certainty, but Mary was far from convinced. She put her hands on her hips and spoke her mind.

"Well that's just not going to happen," she said firmly. "I'm not yet married and so I'm definitely not going to have a baby."

"What I have said can come true," replied the angel, "because there is nothing God cannot do."

Mary was still not entirely convinced, but she let her arms fall to her sides and shrugged. "Well, if God wants that to happen, then... let it be," she said.

At that, the angel went away.

Not long after, Mary found out that she was indeed pregnant. At first, the only person she dared tell was her cousin, Elizabeth. Mary knew that if anyone would understand, that person was Elizabeth – for she too was expecting a baby.

It was also quite useful that Elizabeth lived some distance away: it gave Mary the chance to be far from Nazareth when – as was bound to happen – the news that she was pregnant became known and people started gossiping.

The visit was all that Mary had hoped for. For one thing, Elizabeth believed Mary's story utterly and completely. "It's a miracle that I'm expecting a baby, after so many years of being childless," she said. "So I am already quite convinced that God can do things that others declare to be impossible!

"I believe the angel's words. I believe that you are blessed; and I believe your child will be blessed too."

Elizabeth's encouragement made Mary sing for joy, and gave her confidence for all the difficulties that might lie ahead.

As it happened, the difficulties were a lot fewer than she had once feared: Joseph believed her explanation about the baby. He agreed to marry her and to take care of the child as his own.

So, when the emperor Augustus ordered a census – a huge, dreary undertaking to collect the names of everyone in the empire whom he could force to pay taxes – Joseph made a plan.

"We will go to my home town, as the order requires," said Joseph to Mary, "and there we will register as family.

"That means we can leave Nazareth and go to Bethlehem in Judea, birthplace of my famous ancestor King David."

Joseph did not make any particular plans for where to stay. Bethlehem was his home town, after all; there was bound to be someone who would recognize him as a cousin of some sort and insist the couple come and stay.

To the dismay of both, however, the town had absolutely no rooms left for visitors. King David was clearly the famous ancestor of a great many people!

"We're not exactly being turned away," Joseph explained to Mary. "It's just that the only place that is available for us is a stable."

Mary sighed a little, and then smiled. "That's very sensible," she said.

It was not unusual for animal rooms to be practically part of the house – it kept the animals safe and the house that little bit warmer. And Mary could tell that her baby would soon be born.

And indeed, the baby came that very night. Mary swaddled her son snugly with cloths and cradled him in a manger.

Not far away, some shepherds were spending the night on the hillside so that they could take care of their sheep. The sheep bleated sleepily from inside the stone-walled fold, and the

shepherds grumbled vaguely about this and that: the arrogance of the occupying Roman troops, the possibility of taxes going up, and the likelihood of the local tax collector being a rogue who was overcharging.

All at once, the dark of night turned to a dome of gold more breathtaking than dawn. An angel stood in front of them, shining with all the glory of heaven.

"Don't be afraid," said the angel. "I bring good news: for you, for your people – for all people everywhere.

"Tonight, in Bethlehem, a new king has been born. He is God's chosen king – the messiah, the Christ – and he will save you from all your troubles."

"What on earth…" began one of the shepherds, but his companion nudged him to be quiet.

"I know you're wondering about me," said the angel, "but I can give you proof. If you go to Bethlehem, you will find the newborn king. He's wrapped in swaddling clothes and lying in a manger."

Suddenly a great crowd of angels appeared and the air was filled with singing.

> *"Glory to God in the highest heaven!*
> *Peace on earth to those with whom God is pleased!"*

The shepherds stood open mouthed. It was as if the dark curtain of the night sky had been swept away and they could see straight into heaven.

Then the darkness swung back, and all was quiet.

"Well," said one of the shepherds.

"Did we all hear the same thing?" asked another. "Some talk about a baby in a manger."

"Yes, in Bethlehem. Well, I think we know where most of the mangers are. Though I can't think of anyone I know who was expecting a baby."

They checked that the gate of the fold was safely shut before heading off up the hill to Bethlehem. Lamplight showed them that something was going on in one of the stables.

There they found Joseph and Mary and saw the baby in the manger.

"There's a bit of a story about why we're here," they explained. "You might not believe it, but we came because... an angel told us to come."

Mary almost laughed out loud. "Oh, I can believe it," she said. "It's the sort of thing that happens to me!"

The shepherds told their news. Mary listened intently. What the angel had said to these men reminded her of the things that Gabriel had told her.

There in the manger lay God's newborn king.

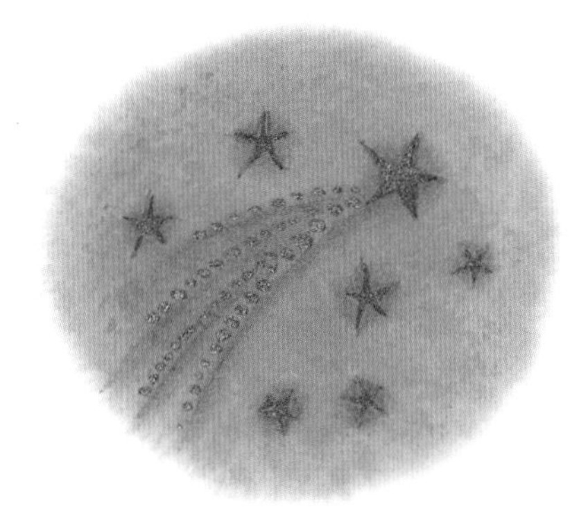

THE NATIVITY ACCORDING TO SAINT MATTHEW

The story of Jesus fits into a long history: the history of the people of Israel, the Jews.

Jesus was one of that nation, who traced their history back to a man named Abraham, famous for his faith in God. Jesus' own family line also went back to a warrior and poet named David – the David who wrote the Psalms, the David who had slain Goliath, the David whom God had chosen to be the nation's king and who had made it peaceful and prosperous.

Many generations had passed since that golden age, and in that time the nation had been conquered by one mighty empire after another. Yet through all the dark times, seers and prophets had spoken a message of hope; one day, they promised, God would send a king like David – God's chosen one, the messiah, the Christ.

And this is how the birth of Jesus Christ took place. There was a woman named Mary, who was promised in marriage to a man named Joseph. Then, before the wedding, Mary found out that she was going to have a baby.

Joseph was a good man who always did what was right. "What sad news this is," he sighed. "All my hopes and dreams have come crashing down to nothing. I cannot go ahead and marry Mary when she is expecting someone else's child.

"There is only one thing to do: I shall have to break off the engagement. I shall do so privately, and that way there is some hope that Mary will not become the victim of unkind gossip."

He was turning this plan over in his mind late into the evening, and fell asleep still wondering if he had made the right choice. In a dream, an angel spoke to him:

"Joseph, descendant of David, you must not be afraid to take Mary as your wife. The child she bears is God's own Son. You will name him Jesus. The name has a meaning – Saviour – and he will save his people from all their wrongdoing."

No dazzling heavenly spectacle accompanied these words. Joseph simply recognized in them something said by one of the prophets of old: "One day a young, unmarried woman will have a son, and he will be called Immanuel, which means, 'God is with us.' "

When Joseph woke up, he made a new plan that seemed utterly right. He went to Mary to tell her.

"We will get married and everything will be just as we have always planned. From the time he is born, your son will be my son and we will be husband and wife."

And so it was. Jesus was born in the town of Bethlehem in the region known as Judea in the years when Herod the Great was king in Jerusalem, just a few miles away.

Soon after, some foreigners arrived in Jerusalem. They had come from lands far to the east and they began asking for help with their quest.

"We are scholars," they explained. "We have made a study of the patterns of the stars in the night sky and the messages that are written into them.

"We have seen a new star that tells us that a king has been born to the Jews. We have come to worship him."

News of the foreigners and their mysterious quest spread throughout the city. In his palace, King Herod clenched his fist and scowled. He had spent years scheming, plotting, conniving in order to win the approval of the emperor who ruled most of the known world from Rome. He had seen off many challengers before. He needed to investigate this unsettling news of a newborn king.

He called for the priests and for the learned men who knew and treasured the ancient writings of the Jewish people – their history, their laws, the sayings of their prophets.

"I recall that the prophets spoke of a messiah," asked Herod. "What do the writings have to say about him? Where will he be born?"

"Oh, that is very clear. The prophet Micah wrote these words:

> *"Bethlehem in the land of Judah,*
> *you are by no means the least of the leading cities of Judah;*
> *for from you will come a leader*
> *who will guide my people."*

Herod nodded slowly.

"Show these men out," he said to his guards, "and then go and bring me those foreigners.

"But do your work quietly. I want this matter dealt with in secret."

The foreigners were brought to Herod. He stared at them, eyes narrow with suspicion, and spoke with a slight hiss.

"I want exact details," he said, "about when the star appeared."

They told him.

"Very interesting," he said, nodding thoughtfully. "And in return, I have useful information for you. The next king of the Jews, it is foretold, will be born in Bethlehem. I want you to go and search for the child – who will be no more than two years old. When you find him, let me know. I too want to go and worship him."

The foreigners left the palace and started out on the road towards Bethlehem. To their delight, the star that they had seen in the east shone on their way and then hung low over one of the houses in Bethlehem. They went inside and found the child with his mother, Mary.

Full of wonder, they knelt down in worship. Then they brought out their gifts – gold, frankincense, and myrrh – and presented them to him.

"We will not tell Herod about the child," they agreed.

"It doesn't seem right. Surely the voice that whispers in our dreams is from God, telling us to go home by a different road."

The night after they had left, Joseph dreamed a second time of an angel and a message.

"Get up," said the angel. "Take the child and his mother to Egypt. Stay there until I tell you to leave."

Even though it was still night, Joseph got up and led his family to safety. They were far away when Herod realized he had been tricked and sent his soldiers to Bethlehem to hunt down his child rival. It was some years later, when Herod had died, that the angel spoke again to Joseph.

"The danger is passed; it is time to go back to your own land. Make your home among the hills of Galilee, in the town of Nazareth: for all that has been foretold about God's messiah must now come true."

The Fourth Wise Man

Long ago, in a far off land, stood a tall tower. As the sun set and its rosy brick turned almost to gold in the evening light, wise men hurried up its stairs. The top of the tower lay open to the sky, and the men watched as the horizon that circled them faded into darkness. Soon, above them, the great dome of the night sky was lit with a hundred thousand stars.

"Ah, they are just so beautiful," sighed one.

"Oh, Ziba," reprimanded another. "We haven't come here to stargaze like shepherd boys. We've come to study the stars… to understand their rising and their setting, to recognize their patterns and their journeying, to probe beyond their mystery and find meaning."

"Oh, absolutely yes, Balthazar," replied Ziba. He tried

to look more earnest. "Now there's that constellation called... um, slipped my mind... Ooh! Shooting star over to the north east."

Balthazar shook his head just a little wearily. He had never been quite sure about letting Ziba join his circle of friends.

"And yet," said Ziba's second companion, "that star in the east is very striking. I don't recall seeing one so bright in that part of the sky."

"Melchior, I think that is a first sighting," said Ziba's third companion, whose name was Caspar. "That is a very unusual star... and I do believe it is moving. Can you see its tail of light?"

The four men gathered to look. It was a new star, they all agreed. But why had it appeared? What could it mean?

It was only when the sky paled with the dawn and they went to consult their precious writings that they found their answer.

"It is the sign that a new king has been born," announced Balthazar. "A king for the Jewish nation."

"A nation better known for its prayerfulness rather than its power," said Melchior.

"Indeed, and for their dream of bringing healing to all the nations," added Caspar.

"A king for whom God has put a wonderful star in the heavens," sighed Ziba. "That is quite amazing. I know we're meant to analyse our findings very carefully, but don't you just sometimes want to say, 'Ooh!' "

Balthazar tilted his head. "I... don't think I've ever had that reaction," he said, rather drily.

As the wise men talked about the new star and the new king, they made a plan.

"We must follow the star wherever it leads us," they agreed. "We must find that newborn king and take him gifts; ones that pay tribute to his future greatness."

As soon as they could, they started out from their own city. It was natural to them to travel by night, for they were long practised in setting their direction by the stars overhead. Now they were following the new star, which seemed to be leading them always over the western horizon.

As they rode along, Ziba drew alongside Balthazar. "What gift did you choose as a tribute to the king?" he asked.

"I have brought a chest of gold," replied Balthazar. "Gold is the emblem of royal power – and can be turned into coins if needs be."

The two rode together in silence for a while. "Have you found your 'ooh-aah' gift yet?" he asked. Ziba recognized a little hint of sarcasm in his question.

"Not yet," said Ziba, "although gold is a dazzling choice, I must say."

The next night, Ziba fell into conversation with Melchior. "What is your tribute for the newborn king?" asked Ziba.

"Oh, I knew at once what to bring," Melchior replied. "My home town is famous for the manufacture of frankincense. The Jews are regular purchasers of this very fine product. They burn it, you know, on an altar in their temple. As their priests explain, the smoke of incense rises like prayers to heaven. The king of the Jews will surely be their High Priest as well."

"Very appropriate," said Ziba. "How very thoughtful – and such a good idea to think of a local product."

On the third night of the journey, Ziba went to Caspar and asked the same question about his gift.

Caspar smiled. "If this king fulfils the dreams of his people, he will be a healer," he said. "I have brought myrrh, famed for its curative powers. I was also rather taken with the alabaster jar it comes in – I know it's only packaging, but it adds a little... what shall I say...?"

"It's something to ooh and aah about, isn't it?" commented Ziba. He had always felt that Caspar understood the awe-inspiring loveliness of the night sky.

"You could," said Caspar, glancing around to see if Balthazar was within earshot. " 'Stylish' is the word I'd use."

"Good word," said Ziba hastily.

"I was rather afraid you might have the same idea," said Caspar, "knowing your appreciation of such things. I'm quite relieved that you didn't. So tell me – what gift have you chosen?"

Ziba bit his lip. "I'm... still thinking," he said. "I was afraid of choosing the same as one of you. I'm sure inspiration for the right thing will come."

But though the journey took many days, Ziba could not think of any gift that was good enough. And though the men passed many bazaars, the goods on sale seemed too gaudy, too shoddy, too... worldy.

After many miles, the men reached Bethlehem. The star they had first seen in the east shone brightly on the last few miles of

their way. It stopped over a little house from which came the unmistakable cry of a little child.

"He's here," said Balthazar. "I must take him the gold." He dismounted his camel and began undoing one of the saddle bags.

"Yes, and the frankincense jar has survived the journey," said Melchior.

"I shall present this very stylish pot of myrrh wrapped in fine linen," said Caspar. "I think a proper wrapping makes the gift – it proves you've taken that extra bit of trouble.

"And you, Ziba?"

"I feel ashamed," said the fourth wise man. "I still have no gift. It is too bad. Let me stay outside. I shall get water for the camels."

Ziba watched as his three companions went into the house. Then he found a bucket and let it down into the well. As he lifted it up, he saw the star they had been following reflected in the water.

"Oooh!" he breathed. "It's magnified in the water – twinkling, shimmering, sparkling! To think that so great and beautiful a star should fit inside this battered old bucket."

Then, without really thinking, he hurried into the house, carrying the bucket. "I thought the baby would like to see the star that God set in the heavens for him," he said.

Then he stopped. "Oh – it's just a reflection. How foolish of me."

The mother smiled. She carried the child over to where the bucket stood in a puddle on the floor.

Then Ziba saw a miracle: the star was still there, shining back at the king newborn from heaven.

"Ooh!" said the mother. "Aah."

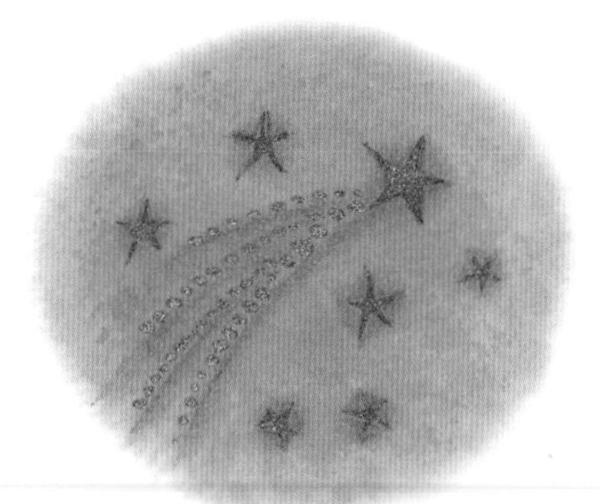

Saint Nicholas

In the town of Myra lived three sisters: Joanna, Susanna, and Maria. The mother had died not long after Maria, the youngest, was born. Since then the eldest, Joanna, had done her best to take care of her father and her younger sisters.

For several years, things had gone well. The father was a carpenter and builder and with those skills he could easily find work. When he was between jobs, he spent time making sure that everything in the house was neatly fixed and mended. Even when the cold wind blew in winter, it could not rattle the shutters on the little house.

Joanna had learned from her mother how to grow vegetables in the little patch of land behind their house: onions and leeks and beans and pumpkins. There were herbs in pots and a fig tree that grew up the side of the house all the way to the roof. She taught Susanna how to cook, and Maria – well, Maria taught herself how to play tunes on a toy flute.

Then, one year, the father fell from a building he was working on and was badly hurt.

"Whatever shall we do?" fretted Susanna. "Without money to buy food, we shall starve."

"We shall have to manage," said Joanna sensibly. "Tomorrow we shall get up early and pick the fruit and vegetables that we won't be able to eat or store. Then we shall go and sell our produce in the market."

So they did. Soon Joanna was busy selling the produce, and Susanna took care of the money, and Maria – well, Maria played tunes on her toy flute; and that made people smile, and some of them gave her a few coins.

"We have done very well," announced Joanna at the end of the day. "Next week, we shall gather more from our garden and go to market again."

And so they did. But the second week they had less to sell, and the third week hardly anything.

"Let's take to sell some of the things we don't need," said Susanna.

So they gathered up the best of what they could spare: a couple of blankets, three pretty lamps, and some wooden toys that their father had made for when his daughters were babies.

Once again, Joanna did the selling, and Susanna took care of the money, and, once again, Maria played on her toy flute.

Only this time, not all the tunes were happy. Each time

one of the toys was sold, she played a sad little goodbye song. "The truth is," she said to her sisters, "it's not fun being poor."

All the while, they were simply getting poorer. The money they had earned that week barely lasted two. The harvest days were over and the weather was growing wintry.

Joanna called her sisters to a special meeting under the fig tree.

"It's cold," shivered Maria.

"It's cold and getting colder," agreed Joanna. "But out here father cannot hear us. I have told him that the money is lasting, and he is too unwell to work out that that can't be true. We just need to find a way to keep going through the winter. By spring he may be well enough to work again, and I can plant a better garden. So we just need to find more things to sell to make money. Oh – and we may have to have smaller meals. And most of them will be pumpkin soup."

So off to market went all but four sets of plates and bowls, the larger cooking pot, and two pans for bread. After that they took their good shoes, nicely cleaned, and the fireside chair that their father had made for their mother when they got married, and a silver spoon that no one knew they had until they went through everything in an old chest and found they had an old chest of rubbish – and a silver spoon.

A man whom Maria thought was about one hundred years old seemed very interested in the spoon.

"My goodness," he said. "Are you selling the family silver?"

"We're selling the family everything," said Maria.

"Shh," said Joanna and Susanna together. The man pretended

not to notice their embarrassment, but the sisters knew he knew why they were selling what they were selling.

"I shall have to go home and get more money to buy this," he said. "Please put it aside for me. It is worth more than you think."

Joanna was round eyed with wonder, and Susanna began worrying about what might be the most she dared ask, and Maria – well, it will come as no surprise that Maria played happy tunes on her toy flute.

In return for the silver spoon, the man gave several gold coins. Susanna didn't dare ask for more.

"How can a spoonful of silver be worth a bagful of gold?" she whispered to Joanna, and Joanna simply shrugged.

The money he had given lasted almost to midwinter. By now the weather was sleet and snow, and the sisters had almost nothing for a market stall: some dried figs, the new stockings that Joanna had been knitting for herself, and some little bags that Susanna had cut and stitched from a long-outgrown dress.

The man who was a hundred years old came and looked, but it was obvious there wasn't anything on the stall he needed. Even so, he stopped to listen as Maria played her toy flute and gave her some pennies.

Joanna watched him walk away. "Do you think he's very rich?" she asked.

"I don't know," said Susanna. "He doesn't look rich."

They went home sadly, having sold only the stockings and three of the bags. They tried to cheer themselves up by eating the dried figs that no one had wanted.

"My feet are wet," said Maria.

"So are mine," snapped Susanna.

"I shall make the fire nice and warm tonight," said Joanna, "and we can hang our stockings out to dry."

They didn't notice that the man who had paid so generously for the silver spoon was watching.

They didn't know that he was Bishop Nicholas, for they didn't even belong to the church in Myra.

They didn't know that the Christians in Myra gave him money that he could use to help those in need.

As night fell, Joanna let the fire burn low even though the stockings hanging by the fireplace were still damp.

Around midnight, Bishop Nicholas came down the street to the sisters' house. He tried to open one of the shutters.

"Oh dear, it's firmly shut," he said to himself.

Then he saw the fig tree. Chuckling to himself, he took off his cloak and shinned up with surprising sprightliness.

He reached into his bag and threw a handful of coins down the chimney. "Oh dear!" he exclaimed as he heard them jingling. "I'd better get away from here before anyone sees me."

The next morning, the sun rose in a clear, cold sky. Joanna stretched and yawned and went down to stir up the fire.

"Quick," she called. "Come and see."

Susanna came running. "Gold coins!" she gasped. "A fortune!"

"Now we'll be able to eat through the winter," said Joanna. "And then I'll have an even better garden next year."

"And we'll be able to have a proper market stall," said Susanna.

Maria arrived just in time to see her sisters counting up the money.

She reached for her stockings. A frown of puzzlement crossed her face.

She reached inside and there was just one silver coin.

"Can I spend it myself?" she asked, her face shining with delight.

The sisters nodded. As soon as she could, Maria bought a proper flute with notes as pure as silver.

Little Piccola

Long ago there lived a poor mother and her daughter, Piccola.

Little Piccola could not remember her father, for he had died when she was a baby; but she had grown up knowing how much her mother loved her and how much she loved her mother.

Together the two did their best to make a living. When spring turned to summer, the mother could find work on the nearby farms, hoeing between the rows of crops. As she worked, she showed her daughter which weeds and leaves were good for eating. From when she was tiny, little Piccola learned to gather food like the wild creatures did: wood sorrel and dandelion, bitter cress and ramsons, nettle shoots and stitchwort.

When the farmers' fields turned gold, the mother could

find work reaping and binding the wheat and barley. As she worked, she sent her daughter off to the field edges to gather the wild harvest: cobnuts and sweet chestnuts, blackberries and bilberries, cherry plums and tiny red apples. At sunset, as the two walked home, they gleaned the fallen ears of grain to add to little Piccola's harvest basket.

But when the wind blew cold and the snow fell, there was little food to gather. The mother taught Piccola to knit and together they made long, warm socks that they could sell in the market. With the money they earned and the food they had stored, they had just enough to live on.

Little Piccola was always anxious about the birds during the wintertime.

"They let us share the food that is there for them to gather in summer," she explained to her mother, "so it is only fair that we should share with them now."

And she would keep back a few crusts of bread to crumble onto the path outside her window for them to eat.

Then came a particularly hard winter. The mother fell ill and was barely strong enough to knit for a short while each day. Piccola still went to the market to sell the long socks they had made, but with fewer things to sell she brought home less money than usual.

Piccola did not complain about the hardship they faced. Even so, when it came to Christmas Eve, she sighed a little as she pulled off her stockings.

"I won't be able to hang up either of these by the fireplace," she said to her mother. "Look – my toes have poked a hole in last year's socks. Even if Saint Nicholas were to come and bring secret gifts, they would fall right through!"

The thought made her laugh. "I shall hang one anyway," she said, "but I shall put my wooden shoe underneath, to catch a gift if it falls."

Having done so, she ran to bed. The mother sighed as the embers in the grate faded from orange to grey. She could not

think of anything she could put in the shoe to make her daughter smile on Christmas morning.

When Christmas Day dawned, little Piccola ran to her shoe. Sitting in it was a tiny bird, its feathers fluffed and its eyes bright with hope. She picked it up and stroked it gently.

"Look what I have," she exclaimed to her mother, "I thought I would have to imagine a gift, but there really is one. Now I shall make sure that my little bird gets the first share of my breadcrumbs."

The little bird thrived in her loving care. It became quite tame and used to sit on her shoulder and sing as she worked. Its tunes seem to make the winter days brighter, and they cheered her mother so much that she began to get better faster than little Piccola had imagined.

At last spring came. Little Piccola opened her window and called for the bird to come and sit on her finger.

"You will be happier outdoors," she said. "You can fly now, and you will find that the woods provide you with all you need."

The bird bobbed its head and flew to a nearby branch. But it did not fly away – it stayed in the woods by Piccola's little house all summer long; and wherever little Piccola ran to listen to its song, she found the tenderest herbs to pick and the ripest fruits to gather.

Grandfather Frost and the Snow Maiden

In lands to the north where winter lasts for half the year, no one is more feared than Grandfather Frost – for wherever he goes, he strips the land of all its wealth.

He takes the tumbled apples in the orchard and the overripe berries in the hedges. He snatches the yellow leaves of autumn and flings them to the ground. He captures the last of the warm rain and freezes it to ice.

"Wicked Grandfather Frost!" complained the old woman to her husband. "I was not expecting him so early this year – but look! He stole into my garden overnight and has left me nothing but cabbage stalks and pumpkin leaves.

"You must hurry off to the woods today to collect firewood, or he will hide all the fallen logs and leave us to freeze."

The old man and the old woman spent the whole of the following week getting ready for the winter and the cruel things Grandfather Frost might do. The old man repaired the roof and fixed the fence and mended the shutters. The old woman aired the blankets and restuffed the quilts and stitched new felt soles on her old woollen slippers. She bought flour and barley and salt and coffee and put them in the pantry next to her jars of jams and jellies.

Then Grandfather Frost sent the snow: cold, deep, silent.

The old man and the old woman sat by their fire eating pancakes with jam and drinking coffee.

"I really wish I didn't have to clear the snow from the path again," sighed the old man. "Are the winters getting colder, or is it just that I'm getting older?"

The old woman sat in silence for a moment. "If only we had a son," she sighed. "He'd be a young man now, and he'd come and shovel and sweep and his wife would bring cakes and the grandchildren would come and eat pancakes faster than I could make them and spoon on too much jam."

She wiped away a tear. "Well, that's not to be," she said. "Let's go and clear the path together."

The old man and the old woman went out. They swept the snow and piled it up on the vegetable patch.

"If we had grandchildren, they'd make a snowman," said the old man.

The old woman's eyes twinkled. "We could make a snow girl,"

she said. “We can make her as pretty as a princess with a fur-trimmed coat and diamond crown, and she can be our winter granddaughter.”

The old couple chuckled as they made their snow maiden. When they added her smile, the sun came out and made her sparkle.

“If she were our granddaughter, she would throw crumbs to the birds,” said the old woman. She went to get some crumbs and scattered them around so that the wild birds fluttered down from the snow-laden trees and hopped and pecked at her feet.

Every day the old woman and her snow maiden fed the birds, and the chirruping made the old woman smile.

The old man watched her, and he too had an idea: "If I had a granddaughter, I'd mend the troika I had when I was a boy." He pulled it out of the shed anyway, cleaned it up as well as he could, and made an ice pony to pull it.

He even brought out an old piece of harness from the shed, and every evening he jingled the sleigh bells and shouted, "Off you go for a midnight ride, princess," before going inside for pancakes with jam and a mug of coffee.

November turned into December... and oh dear. One morning the old woman got up and opened the shutters and cried aloud.

"Come and look! Our snow maiden has gone!"

The old man hurried to look. He could hardly believe his eyes. Not only was the snow maiden gone, but the pony as well.

"Surely she would not have left us!" wept the old woman. She wiped her eyes. "Grandfather Frost must have taken her."

For a whole day the couple hardly spoke; they felt too sad at the loss of the granddaughter they had dreamed of, and too foolish for imagining that a child of snow could ever be real.

The next day dawned. "You know," said the old woman, "I think we should be glad. Our little snow maiden will be safe with Grandfather Frost. If she had stayed with us, she would have melted away in spring. We will have to trust that she will not forget us and the dreams we had."

The old man and the old woman tried to be practical. They kept the fire burning and the path cleared. Soon it was time for

the Christmas fair in the nearby town. The old woman set up a stall where she made pancakes for the children and didn't mind a bit when they took VERY large spoonfuls of jam. The old man mended the troika he'd had since he was a boy and borrowed three ponies so he could give people rides out into the woods and back.

Christmas Eve was time for a celebration, even though the snow clouds hung low all day. The old woman had knitted warm woollen mitts for the old man, and he had carved a new wooden spoon to help with mixing pancake batter.

"We get by," they agreed, as they sat together comfortably by the fire. "We don't have everything we dreamed of, but we have some."

That night, a fierce wind brought snow. It rattled the shutters and knocked at the door and blew down the chimney. The old man and the old woman tossed and turned; not quite asleep, not quite awake.

Then, at midnight, it stopped. The silence made the couple sit up.

"Oh dear," said the old man, peering into the darkness. "The snow has blown under the door."

They both got up to clear it. As they opened the door, they could see the woods in the pale moonlight. There was a troika, bigger than the one the old man had made, and drawn by three strong horses. Grandfather Frost was driving it, and by his side was their snow maiden, waving.

"Goodbye and thank you," she cried.

The old man and the old woman watched as the troika vanished among the trees. Then they looked down. There was a stack of firewood, two pairs of fur-lined boots, two fur hats – one brown, one white – a parcel of bright wool for knitting, and a tin of gingerbread, frosted with white sugar icing, and a note that said, "Dear Grandma and Grandpa: I made these for you."

BABOUSHKA

Grandmothers deserve a lot of respect. It's very possible you already know that very important fact. If for any reason you have not found out for yourself, this story will help you understand.

It is about one very special Russian grandmother – Baboushka. She lived in a house all by herself and she managed very well, thank you. That was all thanks to a plan of work that kept her busy all year round.

When spring melted the snow, she swept the path and fixed the fence and checked the roof and dug the vegetable patch.

As the days grew warmer, she washed the curtains and beat the rugs and scrubbed the floors and put a new lick of paint over her shiny front door and WHY IS THAT CAT trying to lick the fresh paint?

When the summer sun shone brightly, she planted her garden and hoed the weeds. When the warm rain fell, she cleaned out her cupboards and scoured the pans.

All through the long, light evenings she gathered the ripening fruits and made jellies and jams, pickles and preserves.

And of course all the jars and bottles had to be neatly labelled and put in the storeroom; and the storeroom had to be kept spick and span and WOULD THAT CAT get back into the garden where it belonged and not leave muddy pawprints over the kitchen floor?

By the time Baboushka had shelled the last of the beans and brought in the pumpkins, she was glad to be able to spend more of her time indoors. Often there were fine days when she could shake the dust of summer out of the rugs and rinse the curtains to make sure they were nice and fresh again; and she could sweep and sweep to make sure there was nothing on her floor that might tempt a mouse to come creeping in for the winter and WHERE WAS THAT CAT when you needed some mousing done?

For goodness sake, it was lazing in the dappled shade under the apple tree as if life were something you could dream away!

No chance of that with winter approaching: it was time for Baboushka to go to the mill and get her winter supplies of flour; it was time to go to the woods and collect branches to chop into firewood; it was time to go to market and sell some of her produce so she could buy sugar and salt, sewing thread and knitting wool, good beeswax polish and a fine new broom. Dear me, brooms did wear out quickly.

Then it was winter: time to polish up the furniture and shine

the silverware; time to knit mitts and stockings and stitch toys and quilts ready for the winter fair. Oh dear oh dear, there was so much to be done that it was tempting not to sweep right into the corners some days… but dust in the corners was not to be tolerated so SCRAM, you idle cat – here comes the broom!

The week before the winter fair, Baboushka filled a large wicker basket with all the things she had made to sell. She even had time to make the sweetest little toy mice from the smallest leftover scraps, which were NOT for the cat to play with.

"All done," she said. "Now I'll make a big pot of soup for supper tonight with enough spare for tomorrow. While it simmers, I'll have just enough time to tidy everything up and give the floor a good sweep."

She had just made the soup and was reaching for her broom when she heard a knock at the door.

"Whoever can that be?" she grumbled. "It's already dark out there, and the snow is deep."

She opened the door and opened her eyes wide in surprise. There were three strangers, tall and solemn, who bowed low. She noticed at once that their coats – though expensive – were travel stained, and their tall leather boots had not been polished in days.

"We are sorry to trouble you," announced one, "but we are hoping you could offer us a room for the night. We were hoping to travel further, but the snow has blown into drifts over the roads and we have made slow progress."

Baboushka eyed them suspiciously.

"We will pay, of course," said the second, hurriedly. "And we will be on our way as soon as we can – if the snow stops, we will continue our journey by starlight."

"Very well," said Baboushka. She fully understood that it was a householder's duty to offer hospitality to those in need... and she could clean up after they had gone and everything would be back to normal.

"Let me fetch an old mat for you to put those wet boots on.

"And would you be so kind as to hang your coats on those hooks so they don't trail everywhere?

"Oh – and your bags. They are covered in snow. Please take them straight to the washing tub and leave them there; that way, when the snow melts off them, they won't leave a puddle on the floor."

The men did as they were told as obediently as frightened schoolboys and then went to warm themselves by the fire.

"Mind that basket of toys and things," said Baboushka. "I've just fitted everything in neatly and it wouldn't do to tip it up. In fact, why don't you come and sit at the table?"

She bustled around, feeling more than a little flustered as she found bowls and plates and knives and spoons and served a simple meal of soup and bread. When the men still looked hungry, she made cakes on the griddle and served them with three sorts of jam.

"This is more delicious than anything that is served by the palace cook!" exclaimed the third stranger, who until then had said little.

Baboushka raised her eyebrows. "Palace cook?" she echoed faintly.

The men exchanged glances. "Well, we have had occasion to… er… spend some time in royal company," they said. "But that is by the by. Although, as it happens, our journey is about a king."

And they explained. They were astronomers, who studied the night sky and wanted to understand its mysteries.

"Not long ago, we saw a bright new star," said one of the men. "We believe that it is the sign that the greatest king the world has ever known has been born. Not a king who will wage war and demand taxes to pay for the army; not a king who will live in luxury while his people toil to have enough… but a king who will rule with justice; a king who will bring peace on earth."

Baboushka sat upright, suddenly interested.

"Peace," she said. "Will he be king here in my country?"

And her eyes misted over as she remembered the son she had lost to a war, and the grandchildren now grown and gone who might live to see yet more fighting.

"We cannot say," they replied, "but we have heard that this king will be a friend to the broken-hearted. We have heard that he will welcome them into his kingdom, and that his rule will never end.

"We are taking him gifts, to show that from the beginning we will honour him."

Baboushka sighed. "I imagine you have wonderful gifts," she said. "I would like to take him a gift too – well, perhaps while he is still a child, he would like one of the toys that I have made."

"I'm sure he would," said one of the visitors. "You should come with us and give it to him yourself."

Baboushka hesitated. "Oh... there is so much to do here," she said. "I'd like to come but... oh, I'm really not ready. I had other plans for tomorrow. Maybe... I'll come a bit later."

Nothing the strangers said could change Baboushka's mind.

"Anyway," she said to herself, as she waved them goodbye while the last stars were twinkling, "I should at least clear up here before deciding."

In her heart, she was not happy. "SCRAM, CAT," she said, as for the umpteenth time the creature got in the way of her broom.

The cat gave her a pleading gaze and a plaintive mew. Baboushka understood. Even the cat wanted to go to find the newborn king.

"Let's go," she sighed. "I'll take all the toys, so the mother can choose the ones she likes best."

Within the hour Baboushka and her cat had started out. But they could not find the way the strangers had gone. Day faded to evening and a pale moon shone.

She came to a house where children were laughing. "You know, cat," she said. "I could leave some toys here for those children. The king would like that, I'm sure."

The same thing happened at the next house, and the next... and the next.

To this day, Baboushka and her cat are journeying, eagerly seeking the king of peace. At Christmastime, when she hears the sound of laughter, she stops to leave some toys for the children.

Perhaps she will leave some at your house. There are important things you should know. She very much prefers to leave toys with children who keep their rooms very neat and tidy. And as you know, grandmothers deserve a lot of respect.

The Christmas Cuckoo

Parts of Ireland are lush and green and the warm rain falls softly there; other parts are bleak and barren, and the cold rain beats down there all through the darker months of the year and for a fair amount of the summer.

It was in one of the bleaker areas that there once lived two brothers: Scrub and Spare. They worked as cobblers, which at least had the advantage that they spent their days indoors. But that was about the only comfort they had.

For one thing, the country people did not make a great deal of money themselves, and so they took their shoes for mending as little as possible. For another, the peat the brothers gathered to put on the fire never seemed to burn with a bright and cheerful flame. For a third, the roof leaked, and no sooner had they fixed

one leak than the rain found another.

Then things took a turn for the worse. A new cobbler came and set up shop at the other end of the village from where the brothers lived. He had made a good living in the city but now he had chosen to retire to where his family came from. He could afford to live off his savings while mending shoes just to keep himself busy. His tools were sharp, his skills were sharper, and his prices were low.

Very soon, Scrub and Spare found they had no work to do mending shoes. They had to go out and dig their garden and plant potatoes and cabbages just to be sure of having something to eat.

When Christmas came around, all they could afford for the feast was a loaf of barley bread, and a few rashers of bacon.

As they walked home with these goods, trying not to mind the lashing rain, Spare saw something.

"Look," he said. "The rain has so swollen the river that a great root of a tree has been washed down. Let's go and drag it home. That way we'll have a better fire than any of the villagers who are content with their stack of peat."

Scrub liked a little grandeur, and he agreed to the plan. The two brothers didn't mind the mud as they pulled the root onto the river bank. They chuckled with glee as they managed to load it onto an old sack and sledge it home.

Soon they had the gnarled old root steaming by the fire, and when it was dried out, they pushed it into the glowing embers.

Almost at once a great tongue of blue smoke curled around the wood and up the chimney. Then came a crackle of golden sparks, and after that a whoosh of orange flame.

"Ah, happy Christmas to you, Spare!" exclaimed Scrub.

"And to you, Scrub," said Spare. "This is the life. Why, if I were a wealthy cobbler, I'd retire to a little cottage by a lonely moor."

They laughed at the joke and set about frying the bacon.

As the fat hissed and spat, they heard another sound.

"Cuckoo, cuckoo!"

"Whatever is that?" asked Scrub, clearly alarmed.

Out of a deep hole in the root that the fire had not touched flew a large grey cuckoo. It perched on the back of a chair and coughed. Then it spoke:

"Gentlemen! What season is this? Was I asleep when the warm spring came?"

"Not at all," answered Spare. "It's Christmas, and as cold and dreary as the world can get."

"Oh dear," said the cuckoo. "And I see that the place I chose to hide from the winter has not proved a good shelter.

"Gentleman: may I ask a favour? Can I stay here with you until the spring comes?"

"Well, of course," said Spare. "We'll make you a nest in the thatched roof. Come, have this nice slice of barley bread and celebrate Christmas with us."

Scrub scowled a little as his brother passed the cuckoo a very generous slice of their Christmas loaf. The bird ate hungrily and then drank some water, before fluttering up to sleep in the warm straw.

Scrub was put out at the thought of having a cuckoo in the roof, and every day he asked Spare the same question.

"Would it be best just to put the bird outdoors? We don't want it waking up and flying around making a mess."

Spare objected. "It's no trouble to us," he said. "We must show what kindness we can."

At last the days grew longer and the air warmer. One day, the cuckoo flew down from the thatch and settled on the windowsill.

"Well, I must be going," said the cuckoo. "I have to fly around the world announcing the coming of spring. May I have another slice of barley bread to help me on my way?

"And tell me, what can I bring you as a thank-you present

when another year has passed?"

Scrub would have been angry at the size of the slice his brother cut for the bird, but he was thinking too hard about what present to ask for.

"There are two trees that grow by the well at the world's end," said the cuckoo. "One has leaves of beaten gold, and they clatter to the ground in autumn like coins.

"The other is like a laurel, green all year. People call it the merry tree, for anyone who obtains one of those leaves lives life to the full."

"Oh, I'll have a merry leaf," said Spare. "I can think of nothing better."

"Don't be a fool!" exclaimed Scrub. "We need money. I'll have a golden leaf, Master Cuckoo. Two if it's no bother."

But before he had finished speaking, the cuckoo had flown.

The brothers spent another year working in their garden growing cabbages and potatoes, and hiring themselves out to the farmers of the village to help harvest the barley.

Their clothes wore out, and their appearance was so ragged that the villagers didn't even invite them to weddings or merrymakings. The winter was dark and Christmas dreary.

Then, in spring, the cuckoo returned.

"And just as I'm cutting a slice of barley bread," said Spare. "Here, take this slice!"

"Thank you," replied the bird. "I have brought for you a leaf from the merry tree,"

"What about the golden leaf?" asked Scrub, rather too eagerly.

"I have that too," said the cuckoo.

Scrub's eyes opened wide as he picked up the golden leaf the bird put on the windowsill.

"Oh, Spare, do you see what a mistake you've made?" he said. "This is a fortune! This is joy! This is life."

"It's no matter," said the cuckoo. "I go on the same journey each year, and I can bring you and Spare whichever leaf you want."

"Well, thanks be for that," said Scrub. "I'll have another next year, if not sooner. And Spare, seize the moment: don't make the mistake you did last time."

But Spare was not interested. "I'm already happy enough with the leaf I have," he laughed. "A green leaf for me any day!"

Scrub lost no time in exchanging his golden leaf for money. He returned to his brother with pockets bulging.

"I called in on the other cobbler as I came past," he said. "He agreed that he and I could run a nice little business together. I'll leave this old shack to you and the cabbages."

So Spare stayed in the old place and grew potatoes and cabbages and beans. Scrub moved up the village and built a neat little cottage on a piece of land there. He took a fancy to one of the young ladies who brought her good shoes in for mending – and she to him. Just before harvest time, he was married and had a great feast.

While Scrub filled his new house with lovely things, Spare worked in his garden. His beans had grown very well, and by chance a pumpkin plant had sprung up in the compost pile.

"I'm doing very well," he said to anyone who bothered to ask, and he told such amusing tales that more and more people did stop to ask.

In fact, people so enjoyed his company that some began bringing their shoes for simple repairs just so they could stay and talk to him.

"Good company and enough to live on. Aren't I a happy man!" he told himself and everyone else.

The years went by, and every year the cuckoo brought a golden leaf that made Scrub wealthier and a merry leaf that made Spare happier.

The time came when Scrub had no more time for mending shoes. He had a bigger house now, and it needed plenty of looking after. He had to hire a painter and roofer and a gardener and a cleaner and a butler and a laundry maid and an accountant to make sure his money was – well, accounted for.

Spare seemed to have all the time he needed not only to repair shoes but also to tend his vegetable patch with skill and care. Some of his customers found it difficult to pay him money, so they paid him in seeds from their own gardens.

As the years went by, Spare had more and more things to sow

and plant. He arranged with the farmer next door to garden a patch of neglected land beyond his fence. There he grew not only cabbages and potatoes and beans and pumpkins but also carrots and leeks and onions and beetroot and tomatoes and artichokes.

It was perhaps twenty years after the Christmas when the cuckoo flew out of the fire that Scrub came down to visit Spare.

"You have no idea," complained Scrub, "what madness Christmas is. There's gifts for this one and that one, and servants hoping for a little bonus pay, and dinners with people I don't even like. It's hardly Christmas at all."

"Well, well," said Spare. "What a hard life you do lead. Now, shall we have a little celebration together? I've got bacon and barley bread and the most amazing vegetable stew."

The Old Violin

The winter weather that feels coldest does not always mean the hardest frost. Often the hardest frost comes with the chill sleet, slanting down on a thin north wind – a winter drizzle that turns the already fallen snow to ice.

It was on a Christmas Eve such as this that a poor widow stood on the street near the church, playing on her old violin. She had laid a cloth on the snow in the hope that the families who were hurrying home from church might throw her a few coins in return for her lilting melodies.

The tunes brought back memories of happier days: the dancing after her wedding, many years before; the harvest gatherings when she, as a shepherd, joined the other farm workers for a moonlit feast; the Christmases when the farmer invited everyone to a huge party in the farmhouse, where the log fire crackled and the candles twinkled and she ate food with silver cutlery and drank from a glass that was cut like a diamond.

Those days were gone. She barely knew any of the people who lived in the village now, and they tried not to catch her eye as they hurried home from church in their warm coats and strong boots. Only one child stopped to listen, then, twisting off his bright red mitts, fumbled in his pocket for two small coins to give her.

When the crowd had gone, the woman put away her violin and picked up her tiny earnings. The church door was still open and she wanted to see the wooden Nativity figures arranged around the little wooden crib. They were the ones she had known for

years – Mary with the kind smile, a shepherd who looked so much like her husband, kings bearing gifts that were painted red and gold.

She went inside the dim interior and looked at the plate on which the congregation had left silver coins in abundance. Slowly she reached for her own two pennies. She knew the money would be well used and she wanted to be generous with what she had.

Then she went to the Nativity scene and played a lullaby on her violin.

Just as she was leaving the church, a stranger burst in. He knocked the old widow aside, tipped all the money from the plate into a bag, and ran off.

The woman lay in the snow, unconscious. The afternoon sky was turning dark and snow clouds lowered over the tragic scene.

Then a woman's voice spoke, kind but firm.

"Come on, everyone, there's no point in us standing around. Look – I'll take the baby, and you, Joseph, bring that blanket we put in the manger to make it cosy.

"Will you shepherds, please, do the heavy lifting. Get the donkey to sit close to that poor woman and try to move her on to his back.

"And as for those gifts you brought, Your Majesties – can you exchange them for some good food?

"Angel Gabriel: I'm sure you will be able to show us the way to this woman's home."

It was perhaps a good thing that everyone who had been at church was now safely home by their own warm fire; for they would not have known what to think if they had seen what was happening. The Nativity figures had come to life and they were determined that the poor widow should be safe and warm for Christmas.

The little party walked through the streets to where a footpath forked away over the fields. There they waited while the kings hurried to the nearby shop, and managed to speak so convincingly to the owner that they were able to return having exchanged their gifts for strong bags full of good things.

Then, with the angel holding Joseph's lantern high, they all walked along past some trees to where the woman's little shack stood. They took her inside, laid her on the bed, and spread the blanket over her.

The shepherds went back out again to collect fallen wood so they could light the stove, while Mary settled the baby in a basket before unpacking the bags and preparing a Christmas feast.

The kings searched in their pockets for the change they had been given in the shop and argued good naturedly about which of the empty tins in the cupboard would make the best money box.

Joseph unpacked his bag of tools and began fixing the split in the violin case, while the angel tuned the instrument's strings.

When everything was ready for the morning, Mary tucked the blanket more closely round the sleeping woman for extra warmth and kissed her.

"We must go back to the church," she whispered. "People will be expecting us there at midnight."

The congregation at the midnight service did not notice anything amiss, apart from the loss of the collecting money.

"That was for the poor," they exclaimed to one another indignantly. "What uncharitable person could have stolen it?" And they scowled and frowned and muttered about heartlessness.

On Christmas morning, the sun rose in a clear blue sky. The woman awoke to the smell of bread baking in the oven and meat simmering slowly in the old iron pot.

"Oh my!" she exclaimed. "How in heaven and earth can this be happening to me?"

She clutched at the warm blanket around her, and a smile of recognition spread over her face.

Then she reached for her violin and began to play her favourite carol.

PAPA PANOV

Long ago in Russia lived a shoemaker named Panov. He had been in the same little town for all of his life, and everyone went to him to have their shoes made or mended.

His customers often lingered in his workshop. Panov was always ready to listen to whatever they had to tell him. His eyes twinkled with joy when he heard good news; when anyone seemed sad, he would sit down for a moment and think of something wise and kind to say. No wonder everyone knew him as Papa Panov.

But for all that, the shoemaker lived on his own. First his children had grown up and gone away, and then his wife had died. He felt their loss most of all at Christmas: when he saw jubilant children carrying pine trees from the woodcutter's yard; when the women came chattering back from the market with bulging shopping bags full of good things for the feast; when the baker called to ask if he needed any fancy pastries delivered on Christmas Day and he said, no, he didn't.

"Oh well," he said, as he closed the door of his workshop one Christmas Eve. "I shall have to enjoy the memories."

He went back to his kitchen and prepared his simple meal.

"I know, I shall read the Christmas story aloud, like I used to when the children were young. First we would have the story, and then we would light the candles on the tree."

And so he read of Mary and Joseph, and how they went to Bethlehem and found no room in the inn; of how they sheltered in a humble stable, where Jesus himself was born.

"If only they had come here," he sighed. "I could have made them welcome by this fire."

He turned the pages of the Bible to find the story of the wise men, who came bearing gifts for the newborn king.

"I wonder what gift I would have taken," he said. Then he remembered. He went back into his workshop and reached up for a box. Inside was a pair of tiny shoes. "The ones I made to show I was a master of my trade," he said. "I spent so long getting them right. I don't think I could make anything as fine as these again." He smiled to himself as he put the shoes back in the box and returned to the kitchen.

He put a log in the stove before settling back down in his chair and watching the sparks fly up the chimney. He tried to read some more of his Bible, but somehow his head kept nodding and his spectacles slid down his nose.

Suddenly he heard a voice. Was someone in the room? In his slumber, he felt he couldn't move even to look.

"You said you would welcome me in and give me a gift," said whoever it was. "I would like to come. Expect me tomorrow."

Papa Panov shook himself awake. He looked round. The fire had burned low and the lamp had dimmed, but even so he was sure there was no one there.

Then he heard church bells. "Goodness me, the night is over and it's Christmas Day," he said to himself.

He frowned a little as he remembered his dream. "That was Jesus speaking to me," he said. "I wonder what he would look like if he came today? I shall keep an eye on the street just in case."

He went to the stove and stirred the fire to life before adding more wood. Then he set the coffee pot on the top and went through to the shop so he could see if anyone was coming down the street to visit him.

It was still early, and all was quiet in the grey light of dawn. Papa Panov sighed.

He turned to go back to his kitchen when he saw the figure of a man approaching. Could this be his surprise visitor?

He opened the door to see clearly: it was the roadsweeper with his broom and barrow, patiently clearing the gutter. The old man stopped to blow on his fingers and Papa Panov had an idea.

"Come in," he called. "I have hot coffee ready, and some bread and cheese too."

The roadsweeper's face lit up. "Well, thank you," he said. He sat at Papa Panov's table and helped himself to two cups of coffee, as well as rather more bread than Panov was expecting. He went closer to the stove to warm himself, and Papa Panov noticed that his shoes left muddy patches. Now he would have to sweep up after the sweeper!

"Expecting visitors today, are you?" asked the man, in a voice tinged with sadness.

"Maybe," said Papa Panov, glancing towards the window. "But... I'm not quite sure if I heard them right... nor what they look like these days."

"Hmmph," came the reply. "You can't rely on people, can you?

"But you've cheered my Christmas. So good day to you!"

Papa Panov watched the old man go, and then looked anxiously up and down the street. The town was waking up now. Families were hurrying to visit relatives; the baker came down the street whistling, his basket empty and his deliveries done for the day. He brushed past a shabbily dressed woman who was clutching a young child, nearly making her stumble and fall.

Papa Panov saw at once what he must do.

"Come in for a moment," he said. "I can't help noticing that your boots need mending. I could patch the toe and add new soles – no bother."

The woman looked startled for a moment, and then smiled. "Thank you," she said. "That would be so kind."

28
9
MAROC
80c

"Now you sit down by the fire and take those boots off and help yourself to some coffee. And would you like to warm some milk for your little child?"

As Papa Panov stitched and hammered, the woman came to talk to him. Until the day before, she had been renting a room in the town further up the road. But she had little money and had fallen behind with the payment. Without warning, the family had told her to leave; they needed the space for Christmas guests, they said. She was making her way to a cousin some distance away.

"I can't go very fast with having to carry my son," she said.

Papa Panov looked at the child. "He's walking well enough around here," he said. "Surely he could walk some of the way."

His voice trailed off. "You don't have shoes for him, do you?" he said gently.

The woman's eyes misted over. "I can't afford them," she said. "And he'll grow out of shoes so quickly."

Papa Panov returned to his work. The woman made herself busy by the stove, preparing soup from the vegetables Papa Panov had in store. When the boots were mended, the three sat down to eat a simple Christmas meal.

At the end of the meal, Papa Panov pushed back his chair. "Every Christmas needs presents," he declared. "And I just happen to have one ready in a box."

He went to get the beautiful shoes he had made so long ago. "I think these will be just right for you, young man," he said to the boy.

They were ever so slightly big, but the child skipped around the kitchen, delighted at the noise they made on the wooden floor.

"Thank you so very much," said the woman. "You have been so generous."

She and her son set out again on their journey while there was still plenty of daylight.

Papa Panov kept watch by the window all afternoon. It seemed foolish now to think that Jesus might come. He smiled and nodded at people he knew that passed by. When he heard some children bewailing the collapse of their sled, he went out with hammer and nails to fix it; but no one else stopped.

As the twilight fell and candlelit trees twinkled from other people's windows, he felt tears welling up in his eyes.

"Dear, dear," he said to himself. "So the voice was only in my dream. I think I already knew."

Sadly he went back to his chair and sat down.

A voice spoke. "Didn't you see me, Papa Panov? Didn't you recognize me?"

Papa Panov sat up, startled. He looked around. He saw a muddy footprint in the corner, vegetable peelings in the bin, and the empty box in which he had kept the tiny shoes.

"How foolish of me," he chuckled. "I'm forgetting what I read in my own Bible. Jesus said that whatever kindness we do for others, we do for him."

The Little Fir Tree

Down in the forest, in a sunlit hollow, grew a little fir tree. It was not long since it had lifted its head higher than the harebells, but already it was making room for itself among the tangle of wild raspberry bushes.

Sometimes children came collecting woodland berries and they noticed the little tree.

"Isn't it a pretty shape," they exclaimed. "It must be the best little fir tree we have ever seen."

The fir tree was pleased at their remarks, but it was not happy.

"How I wish I were as tall as the pines and firs around," it sighed. "Then I would be able to look out over the whole wide world. Birds would come and nest in my branches. When the wind blew, I would whisper lofty secrets to the other tall trees."

Even when the sun shone in a blue sky, the little fir tree could do nothing but dream of days to come. When the clouds gathered, the little fir tree could think only of how much the rain might speed its growing. When the winter world turned white and sparkling, the little fir tree could only feel very prickly indeed about how the snow left it buried so deep that even a hare could leap right over its head.

The seasons came and went, and the little fir tree kept on growing. One day in autumn, some woodcutters arrived with their axes and began cutting down some of the tallest trees. They lopped off the branches and loaded the long, slender trunks onto wagons. The teams of horses then hauled the wagons and trunks away.

The fir tree was anxious to know what had happened to them. When the birds returned in spring, it asked them for news.

"Look how many of your trees have been felled," it said. "Do you know where the tall trunks have gone?"

The swallows dipped and swirled over the clearing trying to remember what the forest was like the year before. "It's a complete mystery," they twittered to the little fir tree.

A stork flapped along and tilted its head sagely. "I think I know," it said. "My journey back to the forest was across the sea, and I saw many ships with tall masts that smelled like fir. They were very grand – very grand indeed. From them billowed huge white sails that caught the wind so that they almost flew across the sea."

With that he flapped his wings again and flew away.

"Oh, what amazing news!" said the little fir tree. "How I wish I could be a mast right now."

A sunbeam looked over the horizon and winked. "Be glad you are young and alive," said the sunbeam. "I and the rain will help you grow and you will be all the things that were written into the seed from which you grew."

But the fir tree was not interested in being just part of the forest, and spent the summer watching the white clouds, imagining them to be the sails that would one day carry him across the sea.

Christmas time drew near. Some more woodcutters came with their axes and began cutting down the smaller trees – some even smaller than the little fir tree.

"Where are they going?" asked the little fir tree. "Why can't I go too? It is astonishingly dull in this forest."

"We know," the sparrows answered. "They are taken to the town. The people in the grand houses each choose a tree and take it inside. There they decorate them with beautiful things: gingerbread hearts and golden apples, brightly painted toys and candles that twinkle like the stars."

"Oh, how lucky they are!" said the little fir tree. "How I wish I could be a Christmas tree right now."

A sunbeam looked over the horizon and winked. "Be glad you are young and alive," said the sunbeam. "I and the rain will help you grow and you will be all the things that were written into the seed from which you grew."

But the fir tree was still not interested in being just part of the forest, and it spent the following seasons watching the

wild apples grow plump and red in the sunlight and the stars twinkle in the moonlit sky.

The next Christmas, the woodcutters came again and walked right up to the little fir tree – who was now quite tall.

"This one is a good shape," they agreed. "I imagine it will fetch a good price from one of the wealthiest merchants in town."

Just a few sharp blows from the axe sent the little fir tree crashing.

"Just a little pain," it sighed, "and then my dream will come true."

And so it was. The little fir tree was indeed the finest of the trees that had been cut for Christmas, and it was taken into a very grand house. Servants in smart uniforms came and put the little fir tree in a bucket of sand and then wrapped the container in green cloth that was softer and lovelier than springtime grass. A pretty lady came and decorated the tree with gingerbread hearts and golden apples, brightly painted toys and striped candy canes, tiny sleigh bells and slender candles. A servant came and fastened a tinsel star to the top of the little fir tree, and then he lit the candles.

"This is my dream!" sighed the little fir tree. "Everything is even more perfect than I could have imagined."

Almost at once, the children burst in, chattering and laughing. They danced around the tree, singing and clapping – and very nearly toppled it over. Then the servant came and put out all the candles and the children hurried to snatch toys and sweets from the tree.

"Oh dear, oh dear," said the little fir tree, and "Ouch" as a branch was roughly snapped. "Surely I cannot have been dressed so royally for such a brief moment."

But now the children played hardly any attention to the tree. A man with twinkling eyes and a hearty laugh arrived calling, "Story time, my dears – gather round me and listen."

He told a story of Humpty Dumpty, who suffered a terrible fall that threatened to be the end of him. The king's daughter came and found him; she mended him and married him and they lived happily ever after.

"Now let me think," said the little fir tree to itself. "The story has a hidden meaning: I too have suffered a fall, but there will be a happy ending beyond my dreams."

But the following morning, no princess came: only two servants

who tore off all the little fir tree's decorations except for the star and hurried him up many flights of wooden stairs to the attic. There they left the tree in a corner where no sunbeam shone.

After many hours of silence, two mice crept near and whispered to each other.

"I can guess what you're saying about how wretched and ugly I look," announced the little fir tree. "But I can tell a story that will surprise you."

He told the mice the story of Humpty Dumpty. "And that," he said, "fired my imagination with dreams of what is in store for me."

For several weeks the little fir tree waited. It did not see the sun, it did not see the clouds, it did not feel the rain. At night it could not see the stars, and the only glitter in the attic was that of the battered tinsel star. In the dark, it fell into a deep sleep.

One day, the door was flung open. It was not a princess but only a serving girl who shrieked, "Arrgh, mice! Come quickly. We must clean this attic at once – and take that withered tree outside."

The little fir tree was bundled down the stairs and into the garden. Servants hauled it over the grass beyond stately yews that were clipped into perfect obelisks and beyond. There, where yellow cabbage stalks and rusting brambles had been tossed, the servants chopped the tree and set it alight.

For a moment, the overhanging clouds lifted. A beam from the setting sun winked before dipping below the horizon.

The Nutcracker

Clara always said that she liked Christmas Eve the best.

"Look, Fritz," she said to her brother. "Mama and Papa have turned the house into a magical forest – with evergreens and pine cones and holly berries and mistletoe."

"Not mistletoe again," said Fritz grumpily. "The aunts think it's hilarious to kiss me under the mistletoe and say I'm their favourite little soldier."

"Oh, do be cheerful," said Clara. "And look at the tree! I'm sure it's the tallest we've ever had. I love the moment when we light the candles and it seems we're on the edge of a once-a-year world where everything is perfect."

"I suppose so," said Fritz. "But then Papa insists we sing a carol before we have presents. You will help me sing it fast, won't you,

Clara? It's presents I'm longing for; and Godfather Drosselmeyer does bring the best."

Happily, there was no more time for this bickering. First came a loud and enthusiastic rat-tat-tat at the door, and then the relatives came streaming in: aunts and uncles and swarms of cousins – first cousins, second cousins, grown-up cousins, and newborn baby cousins. Clara had been told to curtsey and Fritz to bow as they greeted their guests, but that was soon forgotten amid all the laughing and hugging and, as Fritz had rightly predicted, kissing.

Then the candles were lit, and the carol was sung – all five verses, rather respectfully. Fritz was afraid that a bevy of aunts were just about to start another when Godfather Drosselmeyer came in laughing merrily. He carried with him a huge sackful of toys, each artfully wrapped and tagged with the name of the person for whom it was intended.

For the boys there were racquets and balls and toy soldiers and bugles and drums… and Fritz got a proper brass trumpet of his own, which he blew very loudly.

For the girls there were dolls and musical boxes and necklaces and beaded slippers. For Clara, there was also a magnificent nutcracker painted to look like a solder with a wide mouth that could crack walnuts and brazil nuts with military efficiency.

Clara sat popping nuts into her mouth and making friends with her new nutcracker. Fritz paused from leading a marching band of cousins to glare at her.

He put down his trumpet and let the band march on. He went up to Clara and simpered, "Oh, can I see?" before snatching the

nutcracker and saying, "It's a soldier so it must be for me."

"Give it back," pleaded Clara, pleading in this case including gripping her brother very tightly by the hand in a way that hurt.

"Here, catch," said Fritz, tossing the nutcracker to the tallest drummer, who threw it to a bugler who threw it aimlessly so that it hit the piano with a terrifying *brannnng*.

"My poor Nutcracker," wailed Clara. "Look! He's come apart!" A dark shadow crossed her face, as she briefly thought of inflicting the same injury on Fritz; instead, she just burst into tears.

"There, there," said Godfather Drosselmeyer. "Don't cry, Clara. I'll bandage Captain Nutcracker for now, and I'll have him mended by the morning."

"And look here," said one of the grown-up cousins. "My present came out of a box. It can be a bed for a wounded soldier with nice tissue-paper sheets."

Then one of the cooks came around with plates of cookies in the shapes of bells and toys and stars, and the party mood returned. After that were games, and Fritz even let Clara win a race – when probably it could really have been him – and after that turned a sweet wrapping into a medal "for gallantry in action", which he fixed to the bed of the injured Captain Nutcracker.

As the grandfather clock chimed a quarter to ten, the aunts and uncles and cousins began gathering up their coats and saying their goodbyes while the servants put out the candles and Fritz argued for a large sum of money from Godfather Drosselmeyer if he went to bed right away. Clara went over to her poor injured Nutcracker to check that he was still in one piece – well, two actually – and sang him a goodnight song.

Somehow she fell asleep unnoticed – right by the tree. She awoke to the midnight chimes from the grandfather clock. She blinked her eyes open – but what had happened to the magical Christmas world? Perhaps it really was magic, for now the tree seemed as tall as a forest giant, and the toy soldiers as grown up as her uncles.

From behind the wainscot came a terrifying sight: a marching band of mouse drummers and buglers led out an army of mouse

soldiers, in bright red uniforms with brass buttons. Then, to a stirring fanfare, the Mouse King stepped into the room, a sword held aloft.

"We have come to take Princess Clara to our realm," he shrieked.

Clara gasped. But beside her Captain Nutcracker stepped up and saluted.

"Men, to arms: we must defend the Princess," he cried.

At once the toy soldiers stood up and hurried into battle formation.

"Charge!" cried the Mouse King.

Clara watched fearfully as the battle raged. Some of the toy soldiers were so badly hurt that they lay quite still on the ground while their comrades fought on. Yet many of the fighters in the mouse regiments were cowards, for they fled behind the wainscot while others fought to fill their knapsacks with broken cookies before racing away with this stolen booty.

After a while Clara realized the noise had almost abated. In the centre of the room the gallant Nutcracker was fighting the Mouse King. But he was losing ground! Of course – he was injured.

Clara knew she must do something… but what? Then on impulse, she took off her slipper and threw it at the Mouse King. He was stunned for just long enough. Captain Nutcracker claimed the victory, and the defeated rodent hobbled back behind the wainscot.

"Thank goodness!" sighed Clara, and she sat on the box bed.

As she did so, she heard the sound of a music box. The box bed turned into a sleigh, and Captain Nutcracker harnessed up one of the toy horses that had lost his soldier. He brought Clara the slipper that had brought them victory, settled himself beside her, and shook the reins.

At once the sleigh started out past the tree and into a snowy forest hung with icicles and diamond frost. On and on they went, to where a waterfall was frozen into a crystal pillar.

Captain Nutcracker helped Clara out of the sleigh and together they walked into the chamber behind the waterfall.

A crowd of little people gathered around excitedly. Clara rubbed her eyes. They looked like gingerbread boys and girls, only they were real as well.

"The party is ready," they said. "Would you like to watch the dances while you have some refreshment?"

Clara was taken to a soft chair covered in ruched silk that somehow reminded her of whipped cream, while Captain Nutcracker settled into a leather chair the colour of chocolate fudge.

The gingerbread children brought plates of sweets and candied fruit for them to eat, and goblets of sparkling lemonade. One troupe of dancers followed another: ballerinas dressed in white, twirling like snowflakes; Japanese dancers in white kimonos woven with pink cherry blossom, swirling their parasols and singing as they stepped and turned and smiled and bowed; Russian dancers in bright skirts, whirling and clapping and laughing and whooping.

Clara lost all sense of time as the wonderful party went on. Then the dancers left the floor and the musicians played a few bars of a waltz.

"Oh, the last dance is for us," said Captain Nutcracker.

Clara pulled on her new beaded slippers and struck her very best dancing pose, just as her dancing teacher had taught. They whirled around the floor together, never missing a step…

… until the grandfather clock broke into the music with the chimes it always played before the hour.

"Oh, don't let the party be over!" exclaimed Clara.

But the clock solemnly chimed eight o'clock. Clara opened her eyes to find herself in her own bed, in a tangle of sheets that somehow reminded her of whipped cream.

Fritz came marching in and gave a little fanfare on his new trumpet.

"I got up early to help Godfather mend the Nutcracker," he said.

"He's yours for ever."

About the Stories

The Nativity according to Saint Luke

The traditional Nativity story – the subject of plays and pageants – is actually a combination of two stories from the Bible. One of these is in the opening chapters of the Gospel of Luke. Luke first heard the news about Jesus from his followers – some time after Jesus' crucifixion, when they believed that the miracle of the resurrection had opened the way for all people to be part of God's unseen kingdom. Luke's account reflects this sense of the miraculous on earth. Jesus' birth is among the poor and humble, to bring such people into God's heaven.

The Nativity according to Saint Matthew

The Gospel of Matthew tells the story of the wise men bringing gifts to the child Jesus. The writer, like Luke, sets his story firmly in time and place. At the same time, it is full of symbolism and meaning. The writer's clear purpose is to show that Jesus is the fulfilment of God's ancient promise to the Jewish nation. Everything that happens has been foretold. Readers are not left in doubt that the writer wants them to believe that Jesus really is God's chosen king, the messiah, the Christ.

The Fourth Wise Man

The Bible story of the wise men and their gifts comes from the Gospel of Matthew. In fact, the Bible account does not mention three wise men – only three gifts. The possibility of a fourth wise man has given rise to several legends. This one, from France, is among the most charming, showing, as it does, that the finest gifts are only a reflection of the glory of heaven.

Saint Nicholas

The story of Saint Nicholas of Myra is set out in a medieval text, *The Golden Legend* by Jacobus de Voragine. His account sets the framework of a Christian bishop, Nicholas, who gives gifts to three sisters to save them from the horrors of poverty. The tale has been retold with countless variations in which Saint Nicholas becomes the much-loved "Santa Claus". This retelling gives the rather dark legend a suitable Christmassy interpretation.

Little Piccola

This story, apparently set in France, is in fact inspired by some verses of Celia Thaxter (1835–94), an American poet. Although Thaxter's writings is full of the melodrama and sentimentality of her era, it also reflects her love of the natural world and her respect for it. This retelling extends that aspect of the original, making it a tale about the wisdom of living peaceably with the natural world.

Grandfather Frost and the Snow Maiden

Grandfather Frost – *Ded Moroz* in Russian – is a traditional character in the folk stories of Russia, and the secret gift-giver of the Christmas season. The Snow Maiden – *Snegurochka* – is said to be his granddaughter and the one who helps him in his task. Some of the folk versions of this tale are dark and tragic, but this one weaves traditional elements into very much a Christmas tale of dreams coming true in unexpected ways.

Baboushka

Baboushka is the Russian word for "grandmother", and this delightful story links the gift-giving of the festive season to the love of grandmothers everywhere for their grandchildren. It is also a reminder of what Jesus said to his followers: that they must stop worrying about everyday things and set their hearts on becoming part of his kingdom.

The Christmas Cuckoo

Frances Browne (1816–79) was born in Ireland and became well-known for her warm-hearted tales. The Christmas Cuckoo is clearly influenced by her memories of the life of country people in Galway, and this adaptation squarely sets the story in that environment. Browne was deeply religious, and this story reflects one of the Bible's proverbs: "Better to eat a dry crust of bread with peace of mind than to have a banquet in a house full of trouble" (Proverbs 17:1).

The Old Violin

In the Bible is a story of Jesus watching as the rich bring gifts of money to the Temple collecting boxes. Then a poor widow offers two coins. "Look at that!" he exclaims in indignation. "The rich have given a little of their wealth, but that poor woman has given everything she had."

In this archetypal Christmas story, matters are set right.

Papa Panov

The idea for this story came from a French preacher named Ruben Saillens (1855–1942), who clearly wanted to put the Bible's teaching into an everyday setting. It became more widely known when the Russian writer Leo Tolstoy (1828–1920) gave it a Christmas setting. It has since been retold many times and is regarded as a classic embodiment of the true spirit of Christmas.

The Little Fir Tree

Hans Christian Andersen (1805–75) was a Danish writer and poet whose name will be for ever linked to his collection of fairy tales. Curiously, this work sold poorly when it was first published but has gone on to be an enduring classic. The stories are curiously sombre, and this cautionary tale is a reminder that the glitter and sparkle of Christmas do not last.

The Nutcracker

The original story of the Nutcracker was written by E. T. A. Hoffman (1776–1822). A much simpler and good-hearted version was created for the famous ballet by Tchaikovsky (1840–93), which was first performed in 1892. This retelling draws on elements of both versions while reflecting the kind of Christmas squabbles and making-up that every family will recognize.